Sonnez Les Matines

a play in one Act

written by

J.C. Scharl

Wiseblood Books

Wiseblood Books
P.O. Box 870
Menomonee Falls, WI 53052

Printed in the United States of America

Set in Baskerville URW Typesetting

Cover Design: Amanda Brown

ISBN 13: 978-1-951319-62-5

Contents

Preface · · · · · · · · · · · · · iii

Sonnez Les Matines · · · · · · · · · · 3

Acknowledgements · · · · · · · · · · 105

To Scott, my partner in crime

Sonnez Les Matines

PREFACE

This play takes place on the last night of Carnival in Paris, a city of bridges. It's said that in Paris, in the 1520s, the bridges spanned rivers so poisoned from the sewers that falling in meant certain death. The Seine stripped the flesh from your body. Breathing its fumes made you sick. Without those bridges, it would have been impossible to cross the city. The bridges of Paris were a response to an abyss, providing a way for Parisians to cross the chasms of their poisoned rivers.

We human beings are a bit like bridges. We hang suspended over the abyss between earth and heaven; we are like beasts, but also like angels. We live here on earth yet we seek heaven. We are something entirely new: a physical spirit, an embodied soul. And to complicate matters, it is through our bodies that we both sin and are saved. What kind of salvation would it be that touched our souls but did not affect how we live in our bodies?

That is why we have rituals like the liturgical year, which is another bridge, a long one, connecting the cycle of having and losing that is central to the human condition. This liturgical cycle of feasting and fasting helps us bridge that chasm between having and losing. How do we know we are feasting if we have never fasted? How do we truly fast if we do not know the feast we are giving up?

This play takes place during the frail hours that bridge Carnival and Lent, one of the most delicately suspended moments of the year. Our three heroes (or villains, or anti-heroes, or Just

Regular People) find themselves dangling over an abyss, suspended between Carnival and Lent, between guilt and redemption, between sin and grace.

We don't really celebrate Carnival anymore, and that's a shame. It runs from January 7th (after Epiphany) to Mardi Gras. It is a season dedicated to the body. During Carnival, everyone ate all the tasty things they wouldn't be able to eat during Lent; they dressed up in costumes and performed bawdy plays; they marched in parades and sang ridiculous songs and stayed out too late.

And then, with Lent, it all came to an end. Or rather, it all came to a head, for Lent is really a part of Carnival, and Carnival is really a part of Lent. It's tempting to see Carnival and Lent as separate seasons. But Carnival and Lent are entirely consistent. If we have Carnival, we *must* have Lent; if we have Lent, we *must* have Carnival. They are both indispensable.

Many of the things that happened during Carnival were nasty. But, and this is a significant but, they were embodied. They were real sins, if you will; sins of the body, sins that everyone could see, sins that when people rolled into Confession on Shrove Tuesday, they knew they ought to confess. Carnival spans the divide between our sins and our salvation, allowing us to cross over the abyss of our sinfulness. The controlled transgression of Carnival prevents us from drowning in the poisoned abyss of our strange, subconscious, perverse desires. The sins of Carnival are not the sins that look like holiness but are secretly poison to the soul. They are the sins of the body, the sins that reveal the state of our soul. When we see them, we are afraid; we are so afraid that we may at last have the courage to venture out across a poisoned abyss for help.

Too often we think of these things—body and soul, feast and fast, sin and grace, death and life—as juxtaposed, existing at cross purposes, undoing and undermining each other, but that is all wrong. The Church says so in her Easter Exultet, singing,

"O felix culpa!" — "*O happy fault that earned for us so great, so glorious a Redeemer!*"

So, after all, this play is really just a little bridge, connecting things that don't seem to be connected at all, and I pray it will carry you over some small abyss to good ground.

—J.C. Scharl

Dramatis Personae

in order of appearance

JEAN CAUVIN: a philosophy student at the Collège de Montaigu, Paris. A consummate Latinist and virtuosic wielder of classical logic, Cauvin is destined for the priesthood by family tradition, but his insistence on doctrinal correctness masks a lonely soul, sorely troubled by doubts.

IGNATIUS OF LOYOLA: a theology student at the Collège du Montaigu. The scion of a proud and noble family of the Basque region, Ignatius has already survived one life as soldier and rake. Still limping from an injury from a cannonball, he turns his attention to another battle: the struggle for rightly ordered love in a fragmenting world. Older than the others, and (he likes to think) wiser, he prefers to keep his weapons close at hand.

FRANÇOIS RABELAIS: a rogue, both rabble and rouser; no one knows where he was born or when. Rabelais has abandoned the monastery to study medicine, and styles himself a practitioner of all the arts of the body. He believes that he lies easily and well, and not only with his words, but he values his own skin—and soul—more than he cares to say.

1

SCENE I: *Chapel of the Collège de Montaigu, Paris. Evening of Shrove Tuesday, sometime in the 1520s. Heard overhead, ringing the end of Vespers, bells. Vague figures scurry through the chapel square— shadows thrown upstage by paper figures drawn in front of footlights.*

(Enter JEAN *looking backwards over his shoulder. A moment after,* IGNATIUS *enters opposite, head down, considering the cobbles carefully. As these two come to center-stage, enter* RABELAIS, *running, liberally besmeared with dark crimson. At center stage, the three collide, back to back, and* RABELAIS *and* JEAN *fall.* IGNATIUS *helps* JEAN, *who is scowling, to his feet, while* RABELAIS *bounces up merrily.)*

RABELAIS

Ho, what's this! ah—an ugly pair,
as far as I can see, past prayer
of improvement. Freres Jacques!
Such downcast eyes at this o'clock
upon the feast? Ding ding ding!
Ignatius! Festal bells are ringing!
Ding dong, Jean! Ah, I see.
Sanctity shines upon each face . . .
come you straight from Shroveday Mass?

JEAN
(Eyeing RABELAIS' *reeking clothes)*

You, at least, do not.

RABELAIS

What's this? Do you mean to question
if I could come from Mass all vested
head to toe in blood? That's what
this is, and how I came to strut
about all decked in it's a tale
to match that doctrine which, I do perceive,
you, my friend, might dare to disbelieve.

JEAN

I don't disbelieve, but I confess
sometimes I wonder just
what is meant by the body,
and what signifies the blood.

IGNATIUS
(Not looking up from his search)

The Body means nothing
other than itself . . . My friend,
as I've said before,
you complicate too much
what is a simple mystery.

JEAN

You make it seem so easy to believe!

RABELAIS

Or rather, to disbelieve,
for if I this believe,
that belief makes me belie
the fitness of my senses. Faith! Not that
I question it, oh no! But once I doubt
not this, I must doubt all,
and all else go without.

IGNATIUS

Then go without, and if by grace
you manage to lose all but this,
you'll be the richer for it.

RABELAIS

                            Charming!
A neat use of *hyperbaton* . . .
or was that *transgressio?*
If anyone, of course, would know
the difference, it's you. Keep going!
Perhaps someday the headmaster
will move you to the front of class!

IGNATIUS

At least I know the difference between
clothes that are fresh and those that reek with filth.

RABELAIS

You mean my stained clothes? What of it?
A *stain*ed hood is one slip from a *saint*hood!
Oh, come now, that was a little good.
If a man's farce can't be his dignity,
what hope has he? My farce is not too far
from truth, too; it's plainly low, and draws
by plainness nearer to the truth than yours,
which postures so . . . but why such boring
discourse on a feast day, when speech is least
among the possible diversions! Time
during the Fast for all this speech and rhyme!

JEAN

Says you, from whose tongue spills more speech
than excrement runs from the sewers.

RABELAIS

Excess is dullness. My own excess
is so excessive that it drives me to null-ness.

JEAN

And that is the proper end to all
who care not for the body, mind, or soul.

RABELAIS

Care not for the bod—Jean,
don't flatter me. Imagine:
bringing a charge against good Rabelais
of lack of love for all the bodies God has made!

JEAN

I say this: if you tended
to your soul with half the fervor
you now lavish on others' bodies,
you truly could aspire to be
the finest saint in all Paris.

RABELAIS

I preach nothing
that is not found within the Creed.

JEAN

And what teach you from there?

RABELAIS

The resurrection of the bawdy!

JEAN

Blaspheme somewhere else, you brute!
I've not time or patience for you.

RABELAIS

What? Does Jean Cauvin deny
the Creed? The paramount importance
of the body? Gnostic! Apostate!
Your very farts stink of heresy!

IGNATIUS
(From the far corner of the square)

And yours smell of beans and sausage,
which is worse by far.

RABELAIS

Ah, the tame wolf still can bite! Worse
than Jean's heresy? A rank insult
to his heresy! Heresy's
worthless unless it's done full-force;
a heresy by halves is merely coarse.
What are you looking for so carefully
among that fragrant muck? It's quite a rare
and potent blend. I can guarantee;
I've contributed my bit to it.
But even connoisseurs of swill, like me,
don't often go down on their knees to inspect it . . .

JEAN

Have you lost something, Ignatius?

IGNATIUS

I have—a thing precious to me,
a treasure, handed down, trusted
to me alone, and now mislaid
by me alone.

JEAN

What is it? We'll help you look,
though what of worth we hope to find
in this filth, I cannot think.

RABELAIS

Correction: Jean will help;
I have already too much knowledge
of these gutters . . . I say, that sludge,
I wouldn't step in it too deep.

JEAN

Shut up, François.

(To IGNATIUS*)*

What have you lost?

IGNATIUS

A knife.

JEAN

The very one you showed to us?

RABELAIS

Showed to me. You weren't interested.

IGNATIUS

Yes, that one I showed to you,
and by that willful pride I've lost it
now for good, I fear. I showed it
here, in this very square, but
in putting it away, my hand
must have slipped—this is what comes
of boasting! All the careful skill
of patient craftsmen, honed flawless
over years to reach their zenith
of elegance and use, and then,
a flash of pride, and all is lost.

RABELAIS

It'll turn up, don't you fear. Birthrights,
legacies, inheritances, fights,
hatreds, grudges, spats, customary

disdain, all the proud paternity
of Spain . . . it will take more than a jest
and inattention to lose that bequest.

IGNATIUS

Would you insult my heritage, you
who have none to speak of? Let me test
my fist upon your face—we'll soon find out
how much your base-born blood is worth.

RABELAIS

The honor that deflates with such a gentle prick
belongs, I dare say, to a most ungentle prick.

(IGNATIUS, *without a word, lunges for* RABELAIS)

JEAN

Cease! This is no way to usher in
the Fast! And in the very churchyard. For shame!

IGNATIUS

It's true. I beg your pardon, Jean.
From you, François, I'll beg nothing,
but in Lenten charity,
I'll grant you pardon for the insult
to my family and pride.

RABELAIS
(Bowing extravagantly)

The honor is all mine.

JEAN

François, desist! Must you kindle
this quarrel while on your clothes the red
of some other fight still burns?

RABELAIS

Ah, don't assume this crimson is my blood,
for you'd be wrong. No listen here: the tale's good,
and plenty rough, though I've not yet been in a fight.
There are mysteries afoot this carnal night.
And since the Lenten fast is not yet quite upon us,
though her smothering breasts dangle above, and since
the tale I have to tell is better with profane
ale than sacramental wine—Blood, as Jean
here would protest too much . . .

JEAN

I'd not protest some poison if it could
but for a moment stop your tongue!

RABELAIS

Ignacio?

IGNATIUS

The dagger's not here, I am sure.
I'll look about me as we go
And by some mercy chance upon it.

RABELAIS

Well, step lively then! Let's ride
our Fortune now as far and hard
as she'll take us . . . or as far
at least as yonder alehouse. Come!

(They cross towards stage right, IGNATIUS *looking carefully from side from side. The scene changes from the quiet churchyard to a darkened street. Occasionally firelight and voices, laughing and shouting, burst in from stage right.* RABELAIS *stops, and* IGNATIUS, *not paying attention, runs into him.)*

RABELAIS

Interruptus is, of course, forbid,
but not procrastinatus! Let's pause amid
this rut of ours, and have a good hard think.

JEAN

You're sure you are not drunk already?

RABELAIS

I am not. Sure, I mean.

IGNATIUS

I am; we all know how François
holds his beer. From our straight progress,
I conclude you're sober as,
if not a judge, at least a lawyer.
Why this hesitation? Let's go.

RABELAIS

That crowd down there gives me pause.

IGNATIUS

It's only Mardi Gras festivities.
We've all seen worse before than these poor folk
taking their feast before the long, long Fast—
with each glimpse of a mirror, I would guess.

RABELAIS

Why must everything be so dramatic
with you? Is it some aristocratic
impulse to stage choreographed battles
and make these grave assertions? We poor chattel
have no time for these self-immolations!

This way—let's quench your onanistic ire
with ale and sodden jesting by the fire.

JEAN

Rather, let's go this way, down to where
there are fires and revelries to join.

RABELAIS

Oh, yes, to join, but not like this! Shame
to join a merry band that's travelled far
into its cups without having taken
a single step along the road myself.
Why, I'm behind even you two, who
have drunk deeply of the heady wine
of sanctity! I know a place, down
this street and left, where we can feast
in peace and lap those sotted dogs down there
in their own race before we run against them.

JEAN

Why should we go up this gloomy alley
when doubtless there are countless inns down there,
where the only shadows are those flicking
from the rowdy fire in the grate
and the busy tongues of flame are outstripped
only by the tongues of merry maids?

RABELAIS

Ho, what's this? Does our Jean sing of maids?
That's more my tune! But please, before more talk,
I'm parched. My eyes mist; my sight, it fades!
Get me to beer, while I can still walk!

JEAN

Are you still set upon that squalid hole?

RABELAIS

The finest spirit is often found
within the dustiest bottle bound.

JEAN

Look, just there, a better spot:
bright and warm, where we can drink
and lift the burden from our feet
without waiting for some cut-purse
to lift the burden of our wallets?

RABELAIS

Hush, hush, Jean, for here's the very scene!
And now, the revelation: I've not been
quite frank with you. You're here on false pretenses,
and for a dramatic purpose. Now commences

my story! It's here that I obtained
my coat of many colors. Here's the tale:
I was coming down this way
full of joy and light as day,
and at that bend, just where the street's all mud,
I slipped, and went down hard, and there, voila!
I found a miracle of Mardi Gras:
The very rocks down there are dripping blood!

JEAN

You're telling me you slipped and fell
and cut your hands, and dragged us here
to tell us of your clumsiness?
I've no patience left for this!

(JEAN *turns in a huff to go.*)

IGNATIUS

Wait. There's something in his tone . . .
François, face me. What's this, my friend?
Beneath the mud, a pale face;
behind the jests, your hands are shaking!
What has frightened you this way?

JEAN

He's not afraid; he's drunk. Let's go.

RABELAIS

I'm drunk with neither wine nor fear!
Now I regret I brought you here,
if you insist on making of this farce
something more than a slip and a sore arse.

IGNATIUS

Stay. Something is wrong.

JEAN

Ignatius, let's go! No one
needs your heroic prating here.

IGNATIUS

Look, there; the whole street's slick
with it. And ugh, that awful smell!

JEAN

This whole alley's foul.

IGNATIUS

But not with rain or refuse.
See that mass?

JEAN

A heap of garbage.

RABELAIS

A pile of filth from feasting.

IGNATIUS

Neither of those.

JEAN

A mound of scraps.

RABELAIS

A load of refuse. Isn't this fun?

IGNATIUS

No. It is none of those.
I've seen that shape before,
cold and huddled up and small
upon the battlefield. It is
none other than a human body.

JEAN

A body? Here? And we . . .

IGNATIUS

And we here too, and brought here . . .

RABELAIS

. . . by a fool. You're right; I stumbled,
saw it, and took fright.

JEAN
(Wailing)

Why did you bring us here?

RABELAIS

When I met you two I had the thought
to bring you here to drive my overwrought
frightenings away. But now . . .

IGNATIUS

Now we three are here,
this corpse all slick with gore is here,
and with us one . . .

JEAN

. . . whose hands do drip with blood.

IGNATIUS *steps towards the body, but* JEAN *catches his arm and holds him back.*

JEAN

Don't touch it! Leave it be!

IGNATIUS
(Attempts to shake him off)

I've seen a hundred men, no, more,
in their death spasm. I fear.

JEAN

Death belongs to God, not to His servants.
Do not touch that body. What is written
there is not for you or me to read.

IGNATIUS

We have a doctor here—François!
Won't you at least look for last
sparks of life in this dark place?

RABELAIS

No thank you! It's clear that body's dead,

and in these plague-shot days I keep my head
and hands quite well away from street-found corpses.

IGNATIUS

Someone's hands, it's clear, aren't clean . . .
What is writ here is not of God.
Quite plainly, this is no natural death.

RABELAIS
(Sighing)

I sensed that it was so when first I came
upon it: the street all darkly slicked but not
from rain; the stench rising from the cold
ground like steam upon a frozen midden;
the angle of the corpse's repose, hands clenched
around a scrap of cloth . . .

IGNATIUS

                    I do not see
those things from here.

RABELAIS

                    No? Oh, well, it must
have been lighter then. No matter.

JEAN

You said
you did not know a body lay here until now.

RABELAIS

Did I? It's hard to say just what one knows
when one's in such a state of grim suppose.

IGNATIUS

Did you see it?

RABELAIS

Did I see what?

JEAN

The body.
Did you see the body when first you passed
this way?

RABELAIS

Did I see the body? That body?
Well, it's hard to say. I do not know.
It was dark.

IGNATIUS

You said it was lighter then.

RABELAIS

I know beyond a doubt I tripped on something—
see, my hands, those stains aren't from nothing—
might that body have been it?

IGNATIUS

You said
before you slipped, not stumbled. Those are not
the same.

RABELAIS

A stumble of the tongue, I'm sure.

JEAN

Your tale changes with the telling.

IGNATIUS

Which
is it, François: slip or stumble? Sight
or no sight? Corpse or none?

JEAN

Which is it, François?

RABELAIS

What is this! Can it be
that you suspect me of this?

IGNATIUS

We're only asking questions, François.

RABELAIS

                                             Why,
say I, would I, if guilty of this thing,
bring you here to where the body lies
and so embroil myself within this crime
when I could so easily have swept
myself elsewhere, and none the wiser? Why?

IGNATIUS

Why do you do anything you do?

RABELAIS

I hope that's one of your obnoxious, endless

philosophical considerations
on the nature of the will.

IGNATIUS

It is.

JEAN

The nature of the will's irrelevant;
what we have here to deal with's the deed.

RABELAIS

Only one letter removed from the dead.

JEAN

This is no joke, François! If Ignatius
had done what you have done, I'd think as you
would have us think. But you—if you had found
yourself mixed up in something beyond you,
you'd do just what you've done: drag others into it,
implicate us all in your disaster.

RABELAIS

Come, come, what is this? Why, I look
from face to face and I am shaken . . .

can it be that you two would ascribe
such deep and dreadful schemes to me as never
I in my grandiose imaginings
could invent? Do you, in soberness
believe that I, here, in a fit
of rage or pique . . .

JEAN

. . . or liquor . . .

IGNATIUS

. . . or touched honor . . .

JEAN

. . . high spirit . . .

IGNATIUS

. . . high ideals . . .

RABELAIS

Stop! My tale
tells itself, I see! So at first glimpse
of an unknown corpse, you two—my friends—
dare presume that I, from some dark motive

utterly obscure and unsupposed,
did murder in his tracks a breathing son
of the Most High and further, you presume
that I then left the body in its blood
like a heap of laundry dropped in mud,
and finding myself swilled from head to toe,
I went out from this profane place and deed
straight to the church, where, coming upon you two,
I did implore, nay, beseech, nay,
compel you both to come with me—against
the will of M. Cauvin, *magister,* mind you!—
to the very place of my foul deed?
Do you find this conceivable?

IGNATIUS and JEAN

Aye.

RABELAIS

Madness! You ascribe to me more maddening
madness than I venture to ascribe to
myself! What shall I do to prove my truth?
See here, to show me worthy of the madness
you would foist on me, yet innocent,
behold: I, bedecked in blood, will go,
and march into that much-discussed tavern
to report our find, for that's what any
innocent would do—by baring my
red marks of guilt, my innocence I'll earn!

(RABELAIS *exits through the door of the tavern and closes it behind him.)*

IGNATIUS
(IGNATIUS *takes a step after* RABELAIS *towards the tavern.*)

François, stop!

JEAN

Did you see how flagrant, how uncouth
the blood blazed out upon his shirt?
What will they think in there? Even suppose
they don't assume him guilty, surely all
will think him mad!

IGNATIUS

There's madness enough
in the streets tonight—if he keeps
his head, goes straight to the proprietor,
and speaks his news forthrightly and with calm,
perhaps his courage will acquit him.

JEAN

Should it?

IGNATIUS

Do you think he's guilty of this death?

JEAN

How should I know? We find him bloodied,
his words even wilder than his wont;
he seizes us, won't let us go;
he shouts of heresy and guilt;
he drags us to this spot where
he tells us many different tales,
none quite easy with the others;
then he takes hold our misgiving,
and, turning it to accusation,
gives it the words we hadn't said,
then plunges off to clear himself
of a charge that no one brought
but himself! You call this innocence?

IGNATIUS

It's clear there's more at work here than we know,
but to conclude that he who flees before
the face of mystery is guilty shows
scant charity.

JEAN

What are you doing?

IGNATIUS

                                    Going
after him.

JEAN

          With what intent? To hold
him for justice?

IGNATIUS

          If I must. Anyway,
to stand beside him, as I hope a friend
would stand by me in trouble.

JEAN

                              You'll be caught up
in his guilt, I think!

IGNATIUS

                    I am already,
in my own right, plenty guilty
of much worse than I suspect
our friend Rabelais bedecked with.
Besides, this stinks of an adventure,
such as I've not had in years,
and like a bloodhound, once I've got
the stench of exploit in my nose,
I cannot turn aside from trailing,
no matter through what foul
ground I have to go. Come
with me, Jean! If we forsake
the trail now, imagine how

we'll always wonder where it led!

JEAN

I do not wonder; I know. All these trails
that lead out from the hearts and minds of men
lead only to one place: death, eternal,
which haunts us from within our very souls.
Leave him to his guilt, and look to yours.
Why should I look for death and danger
there, when within I carry all I need
to set the seal on my own damnation?

IGNATIUS

To set within your soul the bounds of hell . . .
that is itself a caustic sort of pride.

JEAN

Don't try to twist my words to match your tune.
If God should choose to save this soul, so be it,
but I'll not amass more sins than I must.

IGNATIUS

Come now! Don't be petty, Jean!
For something good, let's go and fight!

JEAN

Don't you try to persuade me. I know
you—I know your sophistic ways.
Battle's entered deep into your soul,
and though you left behind the fields of Spain,
you will never leave the fight. That
is the very secret of the soul:
it can never change. How it deceives,
and none more than itself! But what we love
is what we've always loved, and what we are
is what we love. And you, you warrior
of Loyola, rake and soldier, jaunty,
proud—yes, I see how you have tried
to change, to cast down your own words,
to bank the battle-fire in your heart . . .
well, I've seen the fire in your eye
when talk at table turns to quarrel. When lines
are drawn, sides are picked, though you bite
your tongue to blood, still then you're most alive!

IGNATIUS

Should I be ashamed to seek to change
my nature?

JEAN

Rather, you ought to despair.

IGNATIUS

That is not the Church's saying. There
is always hope of grace.

JEAN

Grace, yes,
but grace to change? Grace to turn this ruin
of a man, a bodied thing, to good?
St. Paul bids us wear our skins like garments
to be cast off at the end of day . . .
and when I fling mine off I hope I'll find
within not one thing that I recognize.

IGNATIUS

Perhaps you're right—perhaps we put too much
stock in change. Our God, in whose Image
we are made, does not change, and to say
we are free in some way He is not
would be a heresy. But think on this:
once, He took on flesh, He who had none,
and once, He took that flesh away with Him
into the very Godhead, which before
that instant had within itself nothing
like that flesh.

JEAN

Do you say God changed?

IGNATIUS

I don't say that. But it does not seem
He stayed the same.

JEAN

    That redemption, coming
by the Incarnation, was forever,
wrought ages before time and space
began their dreadful turns.

IGNATIUS

       Unchanging, change
accosts us, never changing.

JEAN

      There it is:
the famous Spanish sophistry! It's clever,
but such craft does not impress me. So
the ancients reasoned, and where are they? Borne
away by time and change, into the night.

IGNATIUS

This talk avails us nothing. These
are mysteries, and I for one
will let my Mother Church bear that

burden for me. Right now, there's action
to be borne! I've no use
for those who dawdle, one foot in
and one foot out of life. Come
or go, and with your choice abide,
but send the night watch if you can.
As for me, I will go.

*(IGNATIUS crosses, enters the tavern and closes the door, leaving
JEAN again in darkness.)*

JEAN

Alone again. My body flaps around me like a loose jerkin.
My mind turns and turns upon itself. Rest? Impossible.
Rise? Unthinkable. My soul is weary beyond thought,
beyond decision, beyond action. How can he speak of free
choice? How bid me to abide? There is no choice—there's
only a restless flinching from pain to pain. The spirit
cannot settle, but collapses for a time, panting till the pain
becomes again less bearable than the struggle.

*(Looks at the tavern where IGNATIUS and RABELAIS disap-
peared and raises his voice.)*

These two! These rebel angels, these blessed devils that
inflame my soul! One makes action seem so simple; the
other, guilt so trivial. How magnificent they joust with
error! They grasp the tempter's blade with their bare
hands and draw it laughing towards them. Do they not
know the edge is poison?

*(Falters, begins pacing back and forth, his every movement indicates
indecision.)*

Perhaps that is the truth behind all choice: we are already damned, all, saved only by the dread whimsies of God. Perhaps our error avails nothing.

(Looks longingly towards the tavern.)

If I go, I cannot return to this place. But if I stay, *that* place

(Indicating the tavern)

will itself be swept away to where I cannot follow. All, grasped or ungrasped, is forever borne away. So what avails my choice? What avails?

(He stands silent, as if waiting, for a long time. There is no answer. At last, slowly and reluctantly, he turns up his collar, pulls his hat over his eyes, goes into the tavern, and shuts the door.)

RABELAIS

Ho ho! Our third has come! Our little band's
complete. I beg you, Jean, please reprimand
me once again. Without the toothsome pangs
of your sore conscience, my guilt's lost its tang.

JEAN

Hush! If your conscience does not clamor
on its own, there's nothing I can do.

*(*JEAN *sits in the darkest corner of the table, huddled, his face hidden from the firelight.)*

IGNATIUS

I admit, this buoyancy is not
what I thought to find in you, François.

RABELAIS

Ah yes, you thought to find me pale

and shook by dread of my damned frailty?

JEAN
(In a whisper)

Hush! Not three hundred steps from here
there is a body dead, and no account
of it save that you also were there!
What came of your much-trumpeted confession?

RABELAIS

Well, things change . . . oh how they change!
Circumstances circle round me
like skirts of women dancing, and how
can I refuse a turn or two?

JEAN
(Shocked and furious, half-rising from the table)

You've said nothing yet of what's outside?

IGNATIUS
(Takes his arm)

Hush, friend. Have some pity
on a man's faintheartedness,
and don't fear. We'll not leave him
till necessary words are said—
that I swear on my good name.

RABELAIS

Yes, hush, all in good time, for all
time is good time, delicate and small
and precious as a lady's . . . well, I'll let
your swift fancy see what it can get!
Perhaps another grim discourse will shock
me into penitence . . . Wait, I took
the liberty of ordering for you!
Jean, an ale, nondescript but true.
For a bold Spaniard, a Spanish wine—at least,
it is a wine, and after it has greased
a Spaniard's lips, it will be Spanish wine.
Come! Sit! Drink! And then we'll dine!
To what shall we drink? *To women, wine, and song*
will not go down easy in this throng,
I think, and *to the Church* is no more
the simple joy it was. *To merest or-*
thodoxy? The perseverance of the saints?
The hope that grace may one day deign to paint
our souls like theirs? Or shall we simply toast
that gratuity of God, that most
lurid, bloody, gross, exquisite, bawdy
thing: *the resurrection of the body?*

IGNATIUS

A strange toast, but one that I will make
with all my soul.

RABELAIS

Ah, but! This toast does not
demand your soul, nor your mind (however
fine that is, Señor), nor even
your will—it necessitates your body,
the slow or not-so-slow flex of muscle
in your shoulder; the bending of that splendid
joint we call the elbow; the busy lips
to tighten on the rim; the tongue to cup;
the throat to pull; to say nothing of
the million other members laboring
as one: the heart beating, lungs heaving,
buttocks flexing, cock strutting, gut
burbling, nostrils sucking, trunk holding,
eyes beaming, ears hoarding, skin
containing, defining, defending, maintaining,
holding the frontier of this strange country . . .
all this, while your tongue takes joy of taste,
your eyes of sight, your ears of song, all this . . .
can you do it? Can you raise this toast,
Ignatius? Can you raise it, Jean Cauvin?

JEAN

Hush! You may flaunt your name about
this place, but I'd rather mine be silent.

RABELAIS

Too late! I noted your names specially
with the keep when I got your drinks.

JEAN

Why? You fool! Why do you insist
upon embroiling us in your disgrace?

IGNATIUS

It was ill done, François. Recall,
we're here upon a grave matter.
For us Mardi Gras has not begun.

RABELAIS

No matter my guilt,
I will not miss my feast!

JEAN

You're no fool, but a devil!

RABELAIS

And you? Tell us, what exactly *are* you?

JEAN

A fool, whose greatest crime
was following his devil.

RABELAIS

How about your crime of being born—
the crime no man save one can be forgiven?
How of that black mark running through the soul
like treacle through sweet Easter bread? Dung
runs even from the ass of decent men.
And if you stop the flow, what's left? Death!

IGNATIUS

Leave him alone. It's not his crime
that we must speak of now.

RABELAIS

                              Isn't it?
Shall I tell him, Jean, or will you?

IGNATIUS

Tell me what?

RABELAIS

                    Oh, I'd rather hear
the story from your lips, Jean! I fear
I'd do it no justice, and justice
is what's needed here, among just us.

IGNATIUS

What's he babbling about, Jean?

JEAN

Behind his swarm of words there's something
hid, though how he found it out
to hide it so, I don't know.

RABELAIS

I'm like God that way, or a magician—
I don't reveal my secrets.

JEAN

                      Must you blaspheme?
Aren't things bad enough without that?

RABELAIS

How is that blasphemy? We do partake
in certain attributes of God, and to make
a mystery where before there was none
is one of them! I do not speak in fun;
I mean it, and I say nothing He's not
said Himself, or hinted, or said not.

JEAN

To speak of God as a cheap magician
doing pranks to beguile and deceive us
is neither safe nor wise. God's no trickster.
On that I've staked my soul.

RABELAIS

                        Tell scientists
and philosophers this news! In fact,
tell the Church!

IGNATIUS

                        God in His kindness
lets us deceive ourselves—
He won't trick us, but if our hearts
beg for it, He won't stop
us being tricked. But if you won't
reveal the method of your magic,
at least tell us your tale straight.

JEAN

Wait! For if it is mere idle gossip,
I beg you for your own sake to refrain,
since to repeat such rumor is a sin.

RABELAIS

Thanks for your consideration, Jean,
and be at peace: be still, and listen on
to what I have to say, for what I spend
here is my own coin, and I will lend
it to you gratis. Indeed, all I have
to share is this, and when with you I halve
it, you'll see how little it really is. Listen:
I entered this fine inn, my admission
hot upon my lips, and thought to cool
it with a little wine, and as a rule
I only drink alone when I'm alone,
and knowing you, my brothers in the bone,
could not be far behind, I told the keep
to be on the lookout, and I heaped
up your descriptions to the very roof
so the good man would not be mistook
and give your drinks—those very drinks!—to someone
else. But when I sketched out with my tongue
the virtues and appearance of my good
friend Jean, the keep scrubbed the grubby wood
of the bar and said, *Now, isn't that*
the man just been here an hour, sat
right there and what did he do but demand
as many pours of wine as I would stand?
Of course I pressed him, not wishing to believe
ill of my friend, and what did I receive
but a description that nearly convinced me.
So I, hot on this trail, set my own griefs
aside and schemed with him: He said he'd make
a sign if the man at some point sneaked
back to this place. So hard did I hammer
the sign into his stony head, I warrant

he'll make it a year hence. So, having built
my plan upon that solid rock, I waited.
Loyola burst upon us like a flame—
no sign. But when our good man Jean, the same,
peeped in, muffled like a courtesan,
behold! the mountain moves! Falls the sign
like lightning! And with it fell my haste to clear
my own name until our Jean's career
be told. And now I'd like to hear about
this, Jean, since it's your ass that's dangling out.

(JEAN *stands silently.*)

IGNATIUS

You've heard your accuser. What's your plea?

JEAN

Must we now give account of every drink
in every unknown bar in all Paris?

RABELAIS

But that's just it! Our good barkeep, though slow
as stone, keeps a handy book and swears
he never bestowed credit on an unknown
face, so help him. This paragon of care
showed me a careful tally on the wall,
marked in chalk, and says it's your account.
A lengthy record; a cold reminder

that all we do is noted down somewhere . . .
the tab for today's a hefty five
or six cups, put down fast. To my mind
no man drinks that like for peace and quiet;
he either riots in a festive spirit,
or he's plunged in cares. But he's not easy
in his soul.

IGNATIUS

What of it, Jean?
Answer me straight: do you know this place?
If so, why feign ignorance of it?

JEAN

Of course I know it! It is my haunt, the sick bed of my soul
which I thought to keep an utter secret. Of course it was
you two who found it and came crashing in, throwing up
the shades and tramping with your muddy boots upon
this, my spirit's bedsore, who blunder in and peer and
paw over the filthy tender trinkets I keep tucked up. Can
a man keep his secrets at least till the Day of Judgment?
Yes, this is my little hell, my private nook in the abyss.
Come in, let me show you the place! I'd say make your-
selves at home, but you've already done so—and rightly,
for that is the only way this place could be worse for me
than before!

RABELAIS

In such a hell, I'm flattered
to receive such hail!

JEAN

Well, welcome, I suppose. We're all bound up
together now, or always have been, bound
up and wound together in fate's mesh,
which is always winding, winding in—
no single thread raveling out, but rather
in, all things drawn in, caught and pulled
tight and held within the ball of fate.

RABELAIS

Imagine, the balls of Fate!
And to think I always thought
Fate was a woman! This changes things!
I see him now: sagging Fatus,
scratching at his woolly balls . . .

IGNATIUS

Fate is a woman, and her name's not Fate,
but Wisdom, and she neither weaves nor winds
but delicate embroiders on the sheet
another spreads before her.

RABELAIS

                    Or over her.
I hear she's beautiful.

JEAN

          You couldn't see
Wisdom's beauty if she stood before you
in the flesh, you blackguard!

RABELAIS

                    Oh, I know.
That simple truth I know, and that may be
all the difference between you and I:
that this I know.

IGNATIUS

               And such knowledge is nothing
to boast of. Jean, you knew about this place
and hid it. An odd lie; a shameful one,
but one I can take pity on. Strong mind
and weakling soul are ever uneasy partners,
and such a yoking seems to be your burden.

RABELAIS

Don't let him escape so easily!

he'll snatch the chance and try to flee, poor wee man,
but yoked this way he'll not outrun his demons.
See him sweating there; there's more there, yes,
and mercy says we wring it out, despite
his distress. Come, Jean! Undress
your soul—fling the rags of duress
off, lest in your guilty stew you mildew!

JEAN

He's right! I haven't yet told all.

RABELAIS

You'd be a tasty morsel
for an Inquisition . . .
hear, my proposition:
you're guilty, soul, and more so
than you think possible,
but no inquisitor
can keep up with this poor
soul's confessables!

JEAN

Hush! Don't invoke them!

RABELAIS

You mean don't provoke them.

IGNATIUS

Come, confess; I'll inquisit you,
and gently, as the soul requires,
though with what seal I can close
this case, I cannot say till after.

JEAN

It is not man's I crave, but still,
if any trace remains in man of God,
may not man's forgiveness too show His,
however scant? I've confessed, oh, often—
alone, and to a priest, and by the altar,
and not once has my burden lighted
anywhere but square on me. How
could it harm to offer what I've done
to you, my soul's own devils in the flesh?

RABELAIS

I've been called worse! Tell on. Pay up,
good Jean; I swear your words will stand
in this court as legal tender.

IGNATIUS

                              Tell on,
but only if your conscience bids. Else,
save it for the confessional.

JEAN

It's little.
Here I sat, not quite fully sodden
in my spirit, the dread mysteries
a crushing weight, and here I heard, even
from there, that very seat, I heard—a cry,
not loud, but loud enough, that should have pricked
me to the quick but could scarce penetrate—
yet in spite of all, I heard, clear as bells
of consecration on my ears, a cry, cut off,
one shout for help. Then nothing. Before my wits
could cut their way through thought, t'was gone.
But when that broken body I beheld,
my spirit reeled, for once again I heard
that cry for help and once again I turned
away. What guilt is mine! That I, by one movement
might have saved . . .

(JEAN *falls silent and covers his face but he does not weep. After a
pause,* RABELAIS *speaks.*)

RABELAIS

Well, this is a turn that even I
did not suspicion to suspect.

IGNATIUS

Pure Jean! Pure, accusatory Jean!
It's clear we're deeper sunk in this
than any of us three imagined.

RABELAIS

For if the mighty Jean hath fallen, no
amount of care will clear the rest of us!

IGNATIUS

We pick the scab, and fouler grows
the wound. Each step just sinks us deeper
in the mire. Therefore I dread
to say what I will say, for what foul depths
we have not reached I don't aspire to say . . .
but this I say: by some chance, we three
have fallen deeply in this death. And I
could not walk easily beside myself
on the morrow did I not hazard now
one more look, one final inquisition
of this body—clues for justice, maybe,
or even just to find a name for which
to offer up our prayers. Who's with me?
Who will come and face this death with me?

*(*IGNATIUS *takes from his belt a candle and lights it at one of the
candles in the tavern.)*

JEAN

I will do nothing to escape my guilt
which is as real as if I wielded the fateful blade
myself. If by my gaze even one atom
of this world may be less damned, I'd look
all my day full in the mouth of Hell.

RABELAIS

Of course I'll go! Would I miss this next
act of our strange drama, where I expect
we'll find the dead shall rise or shall not rise,
the moon is blood or merely a virgin,
and we'll know once for all or not at all
what mean these bodies we are born with.
Would I miss this?
Not for all France,
or an eternity of bliss!

(The three exit the tavern. It is dark, but offstage the sounds and fires of Carnival continue. IGNATIUS holds the candle, which seems very small and pale. RABELAIS shivers and pulls his cloak around himself, looking around.)

RABELAIS

I spoke boldly then, and rather well, but I see now
it was the wine that spoke, not me. Someone else, please,
take the lead . . . the streets themselves are hell tonight,
the emptiness cluttered with the specter
of what lies before us all. The streets walk
with death! Someone, please! Lead!

IGNATIUS

François, I'm shocked—if I had to guess
your pet heresy, superstition were not it.

RABELAIS

You had me pegged as doubter,
didn't you? But even the most faithful
can't deny his debt to Doubting Thomas—
because he did, how many of us need not
spar our bout with doubt? But no, I am devout
in my own way. Don't begrudge me
my Frankish fantasies. Up here,
where winter deaths do not decay
but merely freeze and thaw until
the flesh binds the bones like cords
to the cold earth, up here we know
how hideous it will be on the Last Day,
and even if it lasts but half a moment—
that haunted harvest where all flesh congeals
around bones long crushed to dust—
The resurrection of the body's awful,
yes, and dread. I hope I will be raised last
and will miss all your rank regenerations.

*(During this speech they have crossed the stage, then JEAN raises his
hand to signal "stop".)*

JEAN

We're here.

IGNATIUS

I see it: that vague
dark patch low, just at the curve of the street.

It's still there. I half-expected it would be gone.
Come.

(They gather round, and IGNATIUS *holds the candle to the corpse.)*

Look!

RABELAIS

And how did I miss this?

JEAN

The cry! I almost thought . . .

IGNATIUS

Behold,
it is no man!

RABELAIS

Bone of my bone, flesh
of my flesh—and yours too, you filthy celibates.
It is our mother, our companion, our boon:
it is a woman.

RABELAIS

"And Ham looked on the body of his mother,
naked."

IGNATIUS

A woman? How's this? This, the step past
tragedy I did not foresee, the deeper depth,
the darker dark! Always there is worse
that we have image of.

JEAN

A woman. I wondered,
when I heard that cry from the befuzzle-
ment of my dregs, at its pitch and pierce . . .
and all my wonder now resolves as dread.

RABELAIS

A woman!

JEAN

Say no more—no more

obscenity is needed here.

RABELAIS

Oh hush! I warrant I know more of woman
than you boobies, and with purer intent.
Recall, I am a doctor trained; all
my fleshly fascination is forensic
at its core; my loves are scientific
as well as succulent. There is an expert
eye in this head yet, and that sees much.

JEAN
(Covering the body with his cloak)

This maid deserves in death the charity
denied to her in life—even from you.

RABELAIS
(Wrenching the cloak away)

In my own way I give this girl charity,
for I look upon her in the flesh
with care—I don't toss her cheerily
underground like you, who would mesh
in winding-sheets of prim convention this,
her body, before it's long been cold, and wave
away her own sweet carnal self, dismiss
its ripes and rots together to the grave
in haste and hurry to forget. Sure,
she'll rot; so will I. In charity

I will see her, head to toe, and bear
the memory of her earthbound self with me,
till at last one day I follow her.

(Stands silent looking at the body for a long moment, till JEAN breaks in.)

JEAN

Let the maiden lie now
with the decency
you'd give your own mother
though I think this here
is neither maid nor mother.

RABELAIS

Maid she certainly is not, but mother,
yes.

IGNATIUS

You know her then, François?

JEAN
(Aside)

                                As he
knows many such.

RABELAIS

I know her, yes, but not
as you two would have me. Must you forever
be so copulatory-minded? There are
more reasons for a woman's body than
that one! See these pendulous, small breasts?
They've suckled a tiny mouth or two.
And these pale tracks along the midriff? Well,
for these this lady cried out for a midwife.
Therefore: mother, at least once, and in
my professional opinion, more.

JEAN

This is vile, to talk so of a woman's
body in her death. I beg you! Cover
this thing, for its sake and ours!

RABELAIS

Shortly, yes, but not yet. There's a tale
here to be read by eyes that dare not fail.

(He takes the candle from IGNATIUS, *falls silent, and studies the body closely. Meanwhile,* JEAN *turns away, his eyes on the cobbles, and* IGNATIUS *averts his gaze to the heavens. At last* RABELAIS *shrugs and covers the body again.)*

IGNATIUS

You read the tale?

RABELAIS

A simple enough one, yes. Stabbed once and well,
and through the heart from in front.
No fibers in the wound, so she was wrapped
at most in a cloak or coat. Beneath that, nothing.
Know either of you this place here?

(He indicates where, up the street, there is a single narrow door.)

I do—by name only! A bawdy place,
of ill repute and iller management,
where everyone fends for themselves, employing
tooth and claw if needed. I can guess
what happened here: this girl was cheated of
what was rightly hers, if anything
so ill-gotten can be rightly owned,
and seizing her cloak she pursued
the rascal to the street and remonstrated,
whereat he finished with his metal blade
the job he'd started with his carnal one.

IGNATIUS

The wretchedness of it! To abuse and then
to rob and then, when called to task, to kill!

JEAN

Wait, François, raise your light again!
What is that?

RABELAIS

Ah, here is a brightness
that is neither stone nor starlight. Yes,
Jean, your eye is good. Don't touch it! Leave it,
let us see how it lies.

(He raises the candle.)

As I perceive it,
it's a blade, decked in blood as bloody
as its rubied hilt. A pretty toy
to dig up in an alley after dark!
And yet

(He bends nearer)

and yet I think, as I do mark
it carefully, that I know this blade . . .

JEAN

I too bear its shadow in my memory.

IGNATIUS

My God! It cannot be!

RABELAIS

What is it?

IGNATIUS

My God, my father, and my homeland!
This blade is ours!

JEAN

Ours?

IGNATIUS

It is the blade of Loyola! The very one
I lost just yesterday . . . and to find it, the seal
on my patrimony, here, in such a way
and place . . .

RABELAIS

Ah yes, that's how I know it!
The proud blade of Loyola, put
to such a lowly task of assassination.

I am surprised!

IGNATIUS

And I, I am grieved.

(He moves to pick it up, but RABELAIS *holds him off.* IGNATIUS
turns on him like a bull).

                                    Move
aside, François. I will no more leave
that blade lying there in the mud
than I would leave my mother or my sister!

RABELAIS

And yet that blade there felled a mother
and a sister, not all that long ago.

*(*IGNATIUS *relents and covers his face with his hands. The other two
are silent for some time.)*

JEAN

We can pause, but still the question
must be asked: what know you of this crime?

RABELAIS

More to the point, what know you of this woman,

who knows all too well your point?

IGNATIUS

I have no words to speak. I am all lost.

RABELAIS

We will wait.

JEAN

Are you always so cruel, or only to us?

RABELAIS

Always to all of high and pompous heart,
and to you as well.

IGNATIUS

This is a blow.
I am shaken—I, who saw my bone
thrusting from my thigh there at Navarre
and was unmoved . . . Now, by a gleam of blood
upon a little blade, I am undone.

JEAN
(To Rabelais)

His astonishment seems real
and greatly to his credit.

(To Ignatius)

Come, tell us truly what you know;
I'll not be mystified by it.

IGNATIUS

That is just it—I am all mystification!
I know nothing of this, nothing!

RABELAIS

Come on, man! Think!
When did you last see your little toy?
Are we to lead you like a little boy?

IGNATIUS

As I said before, I saw it last
when I showed it to you.

RABELAIS

So yesterday, in the square. You say

you put it away as usual?

IGNATIUS

I thought! I thought! And yet!
Today its absence has weighed heavily,
and I confess during the Mass consumed
my thoughts . . . This is no mere blade for use
at table or in quarrels! This is priceless
Toledo steel, an emblem of a height
of skill that only comes through God's own gift.
It reveals God's gleaming nature, poured
quick as light into the earth and left
for us to find. It flinches not before
any blade; but springs up from beneath
a blow like snowdrops through the ice of winter!
This blade was wrought for Loyolas of old
and for all its long days has remained fair
until this day, when the filthy hand of man
turned what was all good to dishonor.
Do we leave no device of God unstained?

RABELAIS

All very interesting, but I'm curious
that it took the sullying of your knife
to bring this to your attention . . . most
of us suspected it long before, and even I,
certainly slower than most, began
to wonder when we came across that body.
It seems to me a graver matter
that now some girl's bound to her grave

than that your knife got blood on it.
But what do I know? I'm neither
Spanish nor noble; the affairs
of paltry people weigh heavily
on me, and I can't cast them off
at end of day like an extra cloak.

IGNATIUS

You accuse me of callousness
when all my heart's in pieces over this.
I mourn my knife because it is lovely
and pure; it is wronged: the very reasons
I mourn this murdered woman. All things
beautiful are also frail; the least brush
with ugliness spoils them forever.
The good can withstand grim battle
with evil; truth can wrestle chest to chest
with lies; yet beauty must have champions.
She cannot wage her war alone; for her
to enter the struggle is to lose.

RABELAIS

Now there I don't agree. Rather,
you've got it all backwards.
She's a scrappy one, beauty; the merest
trace of beauty countermands the worst
of things and seals for them a spot
in Paradise, if only cleaning out the pot.

JEAN

You're both wrong! What does beauty
have to do with this double obscenity:
the body, corrupted, and death,
the great corruptor? Beauty's withdrawn
herself so far from this that it is folly
to discuss her. As helpful as mapping
in that blood the skies above
the Antipodes as to involve
beauty in the affairs of human sin!

RABELAIS

See, this just isn't fair. Plato would never
have allowed dialogue like this. The danger
of a three-way conversation's too acute.
The dialectic loses all its force;
the third to speak will always seem to have
the final word! How does one knock the third's
thickness? If we ignore it, by convention
it stands. But by responding, we would launch
a new round of dialectic that must
wind again its triple orbit, and that
takes far too long for any normal patience.
Never again shall I speak with two others!
From henceforth, I shall always demand
either one or three interlocutors, and should
I find myself in such a bag as this, I will
demand either that one depart or a fourth
join us. What am I to do with such an idiot
speech as that? Respond? Or change the subject
and let you presume—abetted by the laws

of discourse—that you have bested us?
All I can do is laugh, but that response
would be disordered at this time and place,
so, against my judgement, I defer to you,
only by my silence. But do not tempt me more.

JEAN

If that is your rebuke in silence, spare us
your rebuke in speech!

IGNATIUS

We've wandered
far, yet our feet are planted still on cobbles
dark with blood, and all around the city
rants still in its fever. Above is the sky,
which says nothing but sees all. And within?
What is within us three? I can only say
that within me there rises guilt like a welt,
for I, by the incorrigible arrogance
of my house, did expose and boast
of a precious thing that ought not be flaunted
in the square, and by this I offered, I placed
into some murderer's very hand the weapon
that slew this woman.

JEAN

Sure, and I
was nearest to the crime, very nearly

in the midst of it, but I heeded
the false cry of doubt, and did not, trusting
God to save me, rise to save another.

RABELAIS

And I!

IGNATIUS

And you.

RABELAIS

What strange happening is this! Proclaim it:
that after all I am the least to blame!

JEAN

The rabbit who always finds himself
a whisker from the springing trap,
even if today he isn't caught,
will surely end up in the pot.

RABELAIS

Throwing my own rhymes back at me,
are you? Well, your town-birth shows—
you've no flare for country proverbs.

IGNATIUS

Of us three, I am the most to blame,
and I most suspected you, François,
so I have wronged you most, and most
humbly now beseech your pardon.

RABELAIS
(Bowing)

It is a privilege to be wronged
by such a lordly soul.

JEAN

All very fine,
but the question remains: what shall we do?

RABELAIS

We keep returning to that question,
and it seems God at last has done
with us and is sending our answer
gratis. Look!

IGNATIUS

Lights!

JEAN

The watchman comes!

RABELAIS

And not alone. He's brought fellows.
Well, brothers, let's drain this cup.
It seems our secret's time is up!

IGNATIUS

The watch! This seems too strange for chance.
Someone must have summoned them.

RABELAIS

The devil!

JEAN

Nay, an angel.

(Starts up and begins to run towards the lights.)

RABELAIS

Jean, where are you going?

JEAN

I must confess!

RABELAIS

To what? Did you kill
that body?

JEAN

Not that one, but mine own
and others I have sought to kill,
and that body there I might have saved
but by my wretchedness. No grace
but in atonement, and no atonement without I confess.

RABELAIS

Hey, stop!
He's gone off, the madman?

IGNATIUS

I recall another scene like this,
not long ago, where such a similar
determination to confess revealed
many other truths.

RABELAIS

Sure, but that was me.
I never meant to confess. Mine's a merry
madness, easily contained . . . but his!
There's danger there. Once that brand is lit,
there's no telling what all it will burn!

IGNATIUS

We all keep things close and dark,
but Jean, he longs for light. Even if it cost
his soul, he would behold it. He's one
who, if condemned to Hell, would
go willingly, provided he'd seen the light.
But you! If Heaven were flung open
to you, you'd skip the gates and scale
the back wall as a matter of principle.

RABELAIS

I cannot not resent you and your knowing
tone, but there it is. Be still! I'm going!
Of course there's much I wish to keep concealed,
and the best distraction I can wield
from my self is, certainly, myself.
You're right! I'm going! But not to practice stealth,
not to deflect, and not because you say,
but because *there's* the center of the play!

(RABELAIS *exits, after* JEAN. IGNATIUS *is left alone. He
stands, in a posture of waiting, not hesitating but also not impatient,*

and looks not at the place where his friends have exited, but straight
ahead. After a pause, he speaks.)

IGNATIUS

What a foul night this is! Choices
countless wrung from us, and yet
each one made for us.

(Here he crosses to the body, and kneels, and speaks to it.)

                              Ah, little maid.
What was it, I wonder, the choice
you could not but choose to make?
What the mire that held your feet
upon a certain path; what veil
shrank your sight, obscured the world
even as it made you choose,
not 'spite but from your very blindness?
After this night, can I proclaim
myself different from you—
I, who've long held that to act
is the greatest thing. Action
was my creed; let no fate
befall, but pull it down upon
your head!
                    But where does this leave you,
little maid? Are you victim?
Villain? Was it my careless slip
that flung this fate on you? I have
sent so many to their graves
without a thought, men of action

I hewed down and left . . . but you
lady, you have defeated me.
By your death most helpless, you
have overthrown my life. For here,
beside your death, what can I do?
What action can I perform, what
exploit interpose for you?
I—who've always had something
to give—have nothing. I can only
offer now to stay beside you,
quietly, in this time and place
unmoving, present here in mind,
body, and imagination.
I give the best I have: a lack
of action, which for me is death,
and for you bring all my force
to bear at last on this last thing:
on being still.

(He remains kneeling, silent, for at least thirty seconds. Nothing moves at all for that time. Then, RABELAIS and JEAN enter, RABELAIS running and dragging a reluctant JEAN.)

RABELAIS

Hey, what are you doing? Get up!

(He drags at IGNATIUS' arm.)

This is it; we've really drained the cup
this time. Grab that knife—I know
it's bloody, but let's go, let's go!

IGNATIUS

What is all this? Where's the watch? What's happened?

RABELAIS

Exactly what you think. We found them, yes,
and this innocent, this babe-in-arms, this precious
soul disemboweled himself to them—ha ha!
I'll long recall the sight: this good fellow
blubbering out his tale before a rag-
tag peasant lot who fiddled with their sagging
balls, deigning not to look at him! Reproach
him. I cannot say which was more gauche:
Jean or the idiots he did approach.

IGNATIUS

And they're now in pursuit?

RABELAIS

Ha, far from it! They drove us away!

IGNATIUS

How's this?

JEAN

They did not believe me.

RABELAIS

Said he was drunk!

JEAN

They told me that I stank.

RABELAIS

Patted his head!

JEAN

And sent me home to bed.

RABELAIS

Like a child caught out too late!

JEAN

It is a shameful fate.

IGNATIUS

So explain: why now this flight,
if your confession's gone awry?

RABELAIS

Ah, yes. They disbelieved him, true, but not
entirely. Even candlelight
can tell the streets are hell tonight, and though
they laughed at Jean, one or two I saw
shook their heads. A few are coming close
behind, and they expect mischief, I think,
though not at our hands. Our wild efforts
to incriminate ourselves for something
we'd not done while also treading careful
not to lie . . . well, that dissonance
convinced them first of something rather dreadful
here, and second of our innocence.

JEAN

I tried, I really tried! I sought to own,
without by falsehood adding to the score,
the culpability that's rightly mine!

IGNATIUS

Under the law, you know, that's none.

RABELAIS

As I've said all along! However, should
that same disbelieving crew come round
that corner (see there! Even now their torches
flicker in reflection on the stone!)

(He points at lights that flicker in the distance.)

    and find not only Jean and I, but bone
and blood and this slain girl, and more,
find too the knife that slew her, *and* what's more,
find kneeling by her corpse the man who's known
by many as that knife's proper owner . . .
well, I think that even they would find some more
questions to ask, and more guilt to offer round.

IGNATIUS

So. After all, it comes to this!
How strange that at the end, it's I
who's forced to choose to stand or flee—
sin's wages are without proportion!

RABELAIS

Your speeches always move me, but
a speech now isn't what we need,
unless it moves us far from here.

IGNATIUS

Oh, yes, go! For me, I'll stay.

RABELAIS

Loyola! The torches! Look!
Don't be heroic—this is no book!
This is no game. For this, you'll hang!

IGNATIUS

I care not for my death.

RABELAIS

Neither would I, except I'll swear
you didn't do it, and I care
a lot about protecting innocence,
since that's always my own last defense.

JEAN

He's prattling, but he's right, Ignatius. Listen
to reason. Come away, and let matters
take their course. Don't thrust a stick into
the wheels of justice just to spare your pride!

RABELAIS

Well, look at you! You're as convincing now
as you were laughable before. How?

IGNATIUS

Very well, I'll come with you,
since that's your plea, though in the end
it will only make things worse
for me. But, the knife stays here;
though it slay me, I'll not touch it.

JEAN

But . . .

RABELAIS
(Aside to Jean)

Leave it to me. Our friend
won't be undone by his false pride again.

(To all)

Then that's it; our time has come.
We'll go, and leave justice to find its way
How e'er it can.

(He shoos the others ahead of him.)

Go! Go!

(JEAN and IGNATIUS *exit,* RABELAIS *close behind. Then swiftly, he darts back and pockets* IGNATIUS' *knife. The torches come right up to the edge of view; the crimson light falls on the body as the three withdraw.)*

SCENE V: *A bridge spans the Seine; above, the moon, below, the moon reflected in the reeking water.*

(All three enter stage right, cross to the bridge, then pause, panting.)

JEAN

Are we away?

RABELAIS

        Far, and even more,
we've put at least a few fair troops
of revelers between ourselves
and that grim place. We're away!
The shadow's passed, my friends! We've mined the lode
of all our guilt and found no gems—just rock.
Leave it behind! A tragedy, a shock,
and yet we've all paid our respects as best
we could. You wouldn't aspire to arrest
and trial for a death you heard mentioned
in the street, or beg for swift detention
whene'er you passed a funeral cortege,
would you? No, you'd cross yourself, pledge
a Mass or two if you were deeply touched,
murmur a prayer, and go; if blame could clutch
and hold us fast for every death, who
could bear to live? Not I! Plainly, not you!

IGNATIUS

You're right: there's often little to be done
in the face of death. It is a matter
for God's justice. But you're also wrong,
for this was no natural death. Here is
a case for human justice, and that, I fear,
we have not in our flight contrived to serve.

JEAN
*(In this speech, he is clearly relieved but struggling with that
feeling, as it is an unfamiliar one for him.)*

It's strange; I think François is right. After all,
we really tried. We offered all we knew,
and we were sent away. Don't you think,
Ignatius, that you, the easy culprit, would have
distracted justice from the truth? Perhaps
it's better that we left.

IGNATIUS
(Sighs)

                              At least,
should they wish to question me,
they have my knife—though I've nothing
to tell them that's not written on its blade.

(RABELAIS and JEAN exchange glances.)

RABELAIS

(Speaks hurriedly, growing giddier and giddier throughout his speech until he is quite out of control.)

Well! You've both now said I'm right,
and I won't ask for more. Come!
The Fast draws nigh, we've not begun the feast!
The night's not young—I almost see the dawn,
and in the cockeyed crowds I saw a yawn
or two. Come! Before the night is done,
I wish to raise a cup and toast Manon!

JEAN

Manon?

IGNATIUS

Who is Manon?

RABELAIS
(Scrambling)

Did I say
Manon? I know no woman of that name.

IGNATIUS

You said Manon.

JEAN

You wish to toast Manon,
you said.

RABELAIS

You dullards misheard me!

IGNATIUS and JEAN

We did not!

RABELAIS

Manon? My mother's cousin is Manon,
Manon of many yawns, we call her . . .

JEAN

Stop it!

IGNATIUS
(Suddenly snapping, he grabs RABELAIS *roughly and shoves
him against the railing of the bridge, forcing* RABELAIS' *head
and shoulders over the edge towards the waters below.)*

You knew her, you felon!

RABELAIS
(Gasping but trying to speak lightly)

My mother's cousin? Slightly, but . . .

IGNATIUS
(Shaking him roughly)

That girl! You knew her, didn't you!

JEAN

I knew he could not be innocent in this!

IGNATIUS
(Shaking him again, more roughly)

Say it!

RABELAIS

All right! All right: I knew her.

IGNATIUS

How could I be so taken in?

JEAN

I never believed him, did I?

RABELAIS

But only a little! Let me down, I beg!

(IGNATIUS *eases his grip, but does not let go entirely.*)

I met her once, in passing. She's a friend
of a delicious laundress I know well
(oh, how Aline can starch a ruff!) who, in
her largesse sometimes lets me walk beside her—
only thrice, the temptress!—and on one
of these occasions we met this Manon.
I knew her when first I stumbled on
the body and I fled—my only thought
was to betake myself as far from there
as any fellow could, but I met you,
and then it occurred to me: there'd be
no better proof of innocence than
to return, you two in tow, and cast
relentless light upon the scene. I swear,
now I've told all!

JEAN

             You sought to tangle us
in your sordid affair, just as I said!

RABELAIS

My only fault was stumbling upon you,
the only men in Paris guiltier than I.

IGNATIUS

Save one, I hope.

RABELAIS

Yes. Save one.

(All three are silent for a moment, in a tableau: RABELAIS *backed up against the railing of the river;* IGNATIUS *holding him;* JEAN *a step away, his face a mingling of triumph and horror. At last* IGNATIUS *lowers his arm and releases* RABELAIS, *who rubs ruefully at his throat.)*

IGNATIUS

So.

RABELAIS

So.

JEAN

So what? It is clear what must be done
to end this most disastrous night.

IGNATIUS

Is it?

RABELAIS

Yes, is it?

JEAN

It is! You'll think me rigid, no doubt; unkind,
cruel even—they always do, eventually, all those
who call me friend, for every friendship hinges on
that compromise, that turning away, the slightest
batting of an eye, the keeping back of a single word . . .
For if we are all complicit together, who can judge?
That is what you say, no doubt—that is what
everyone says: ah, but who can judge? Well,
someone, and I'll tell you who: *I* must,
and not with relish but with grief, for each
judgment made on earth foretastes the endless
one to come. But how can I not, when from
this friendless woman's body there comes such
a cry demanding justice that would follow me
all the days of my life should I ignore it . . .
what shall we do? We shall end this thing.
Without flinching. The crime lies at the door

of one among us; he must answer.
If he will not, we must make him!

RABELAIS

Then do it.

(JEAN *looks at him in surprise.*)

RABELAIS

You heard me. No one's stopping you. Go
fling yourself upon them as before
and see just how they answer this new faux
confession. What will you say? *'Oh, I've more:*
before I blamed myself but now I'd like
to blame that other fellow, you know, the one
who came with me. See, I took a little hike–
just as you suggested–and saw I had it wrong.
Silly error, anyone might make it: it wasn't me,
but him! Forget my tears, the wine upon my breath, and heed:
there you'll find the doer of the deed!
What could they possibly find here to doubt?

JEAN

It may be as you say. It likely will;
in predicting ways and means of men,
you're not often wrong. I think you must,
François, luxuriate in the obscene
spectacle of choice—a spectacle

only. In truth, no choice is free; nothing
can be free that is so wrung upon
the mangle of desire twisting, twisting
till there's only one way we can move.
Corruption, rank around us, creeping through
our flesh like ants through earth; our every making—
kingdoms, thrones, sees and statues—all
with death swelling in our veins. And this
corruption you, obscene irreverent villain,
would parade before my eyes with gaudy
ribbons and with music—would have me
laugh and caper with corruption while
my very tongue is foul with it; my nostrils
stink of it! And yet, despite all that,
there is one thing left that we can do:
we can hurl ourselves, despite the mocking
of the whole created world, upon
grace, whatever that may be, and where-
soever we shall find it, and though at last
I turn my back on you and flee to follow
grace not in hope, nor faith, but terror,
I will go, whatever I may find,
and may that be accounted in my favor.
I don't say farewell, nor adieu;
I say only that if my quest tonight
should fail, and we meet again by chance
I think that all will not go well with you.

(JEAN *departs, leaving* IGNATIUS *and* RABELAIS *both a little stunned by this speech.*)

RABELAIS

Whew! Who'd have thought it: him so bookishly
correct, nice in every way and then some,
and all the while seething with such venom!

(IGNATIUS *opens his mouth to reply, but is interrupted by the heavy
ringing of bells. They come from all over the city, and the tolling layers
upon itself.*)

IGNATIUS

The bells!

RABELAIS

Every bell ever made, I'd say!

IGNATIUS

The bells of Shrovetide's ending! Lent,
the long, the silent sigh of Lent
comes close behind. Listen! Matins
bells are ringing, brother!

(They listen.)

         Cold
will dawn this day, and red, and dreary
light cast full upon the face
of foes hid within the ranks.

This is the summons, friend! The bells
call us to confession, now,
before the feast is ended. Me,
I count this night as dearly bought
revelation, realization.
I see pride, flightiness,
and fright driving wild the bright
chariots of our souls . . . long,
long I've slept, long endured
anxious dreams, thrashed in throes
of my own dignity—and now,
bereft of pride, marked for arrest,
I wake, and waking, I exult!
Sleepers, hark! Hear the bells!
What the night that brings such light
can be called black? Hear the bells!
It is my summons; the trumpet sounds;
my general calls, the battle's well
begun! Whatever comes, I know
where my first loyalty is owed:
to God's Church, who bids me now
make haste to be well shrived. From there,
whatever comes is good. Listen!
Haste! The Fast is at the door!

(IGNATIUS *exits in the direction of the nearest bells, wildly but with joy in his face.* RABELAIS *is left alone onstage. One by one the bells fall silent.*)

RABELAIS

That's it? After all that, they've both gone
and left the final word to me! Withdrawn

without a fight! Who taught them rhetoric,
these babes?
        What shall I say, since there's no threat
of contradiction? I find the stage is mine . . .
and now it's mine I find I would decline it,
for what good is it to speechify
without a worthy someone to defy you?
I wonder, could those two have punished me
through any crueler means than leaving me
alone? But I'll play; through the hoop I'll jump:
A night like this demands a summing-up,
whether on stage or at the tavern door.

(Here, RABELAIS *removes* IGNATIUS' *knife from his pocket and
toys with it throughout the speech that follows: tossing it, fingering the
bloody blade, tapping the jeweled grip against his chin.)*

So what's my scene? A woman dead, a score
of night watchmen dismayed; one friend
outraged, another friend embroiled, and I,
Rabelais, jesting as all sparks fly.
Ignatius speaks of battle pitched, and Jean,
he hopes I'm killed in it, but I jest on,
for jesting's still a noble art, at least
as noble as war or reading creased
books in dusty halls of learning. Love
Wisdom, say I, but not with what's above!
She's a pretty girl, and ripe; love her
with your body, your skin and bones, the gurgle
of your gut; love her with your rutting heart.
We're all little pigs, rooting in the dirt
after something—the slut, the priest, the lord,
magister, mother, student, tenant, doctor,
bishop, king, pope—saints and sinners

all rooting in the mud, this slick, thick,
sandy, smelly muck, made up of sick
things, dead things, live things, fat things, fecund
too; from muck, mushrooms spring; hounds
and prey flounder together in it; trees
heave up from muck then willing drop their seeds;
from muck comes vines, then grapes, then wine, then we
o'erdrink ourselves, send back the muck as spew;
from muck comes stem, then leaves, then flower, then fruit
which we devour, then from our buttocks shoots—
and we, poor things, come from it too: that muck
to muck, muck we are, to muckiest muck
we shall return. But we—unlike the rest
of all muck's children—we alone can jest!

So come, Lent! Bring your fasts, your penance,
bring your somber days and long repentance;
weigh down our spirits even unto muck;
I'll go with you, and gladly, and be stuck
struck awhile, for in the muck's the stuff
of our selves: the fair, the foul, the rough,
the smooth—and all the finest jokes, of course,
come not from the smooth parts but the coarse.
The highest heights of heaven are light,
the finest hearts on earth are light;
if He who sits in heaven laughs at us,
what else can we do but laugh *gratis*?
And if He who sits in heaven smiles,
what can earth do but put aside her wiles
and smile too? The world is ours, the world,
the flesh, and the devil—and the world
the body, blood, and mind, all ours, all play!
This world is ours, to save, or throw away.

(When this speech is over, RABELAIS *looks at the knife for a moment, then guffaws and tosses it carelessly into the river. He exits.)*

THE END

ACKNOWLEDGEMENTS

Thank you to the many friends who showed interest in this project at its various stages; to Lesley Clinton, who pointed me to more letters of St. Ignatius; to Matthew Kaal, who was unfailingly intrigued by the characters; to Morgan Meis, who assumed I would finish this thing; to Betsy K. Brown and Tessa Carman, my dear versifying friends, who helped me make important cuts; to Suzanne Wolfe, who edited and encouraged at a key moment; to Samuel McClelland, Isak Bond, and Alexander Grudem, who gave an impassioned first reading; to my mother and father, who taught me to love both art and faith; and to Scott and Leo and Stella Scharl, who make it possible for me to write.

About the Author

JANE CLARK SCHARL is a poet and critic. Her poetry has appeared in some of the nation's top poetry journals, including *The New Ohio Review, The Hudson Review,* and *The American Journal of Poetry,* as well as internationally on the BBC. Her criticism has appeared in many magazines and journals, including *Dappled Things, The Lamp, Fare Forward, The European Conservative,* and others. She serves as a senior editor for *The European Conservative,* and teaches poetry through a partnership with Intercollegiate Studies Institute.

CPSIA information can be obtained
at www.ICGtesting.com
Printed in the USA
BVHW052058180123
656485BV00006B/123